Flower Fairies™ Sparkly Sticker Book

Inspired by Cicely Mary Barker

Every day is full of fun and games in Flower Fairyland!
Join in the fun and use the sparkly stickers in the
middle of the book to help you with all the
Flower Fairy puzzles.

FREDERICK WARNE

Winter Magic

Even in the winter there will be something sparkling in the garden. Raindrops twinkle and snow glistens on the wings of hiding Flower Fairies. Look at the fairy outlines on these pages and find stickers to match. Can you unscramble the fairies' names? There's a list below to help you.

Hawthorn
Holly
Snowdrop
Winter jasmine

loyhl

_ _ _ _ _

psoodwrn

_ _ _ _ _ _ _ _

hthwanro

_ _ _ _ _ _ _ _ _

trienw nisjame

_ _ _ _ _ _ _ _ _ _ _ _

Why not write a poem about one of the
winter fairies. Here are some rhyming
words to start you off! Holly/jolly,
berry/merry, snow/go, tree/glee.

A Flying Visit

These fairies are planning a visit to their friends at the other end of the garden. First find the sparkling fairy stickers to match the outlines, then follow the lines to find out who is visiting who. Which fairy passes over the most butterflies and flowers on their way?

White Clover Fairy

Primrose Fairy

Herb Robert Fairy

4

Honeysuckle Fairy

Ragged Robin Fairy

Burdock Fairy

Garden Fairies

There are three Flower Fairies missing from this beautiful garden. Read all about them below, then try to decide where each one would be happiest. Now find the fairy stickers and place them in the garden.

The Forget-me-not Fairy's best friend is Iris. Forget-me-not loves to be close to the cool water of the stream.

Iris Fairy

Grape Hyacinth Fairy

Ground Ivy Fairy

The Candytuft Fairy likes sitting on her flowers in the summer breeze. She loves the sunshine, so don't place her too close to the ground!

The Tulip Fairy often plays in the garden flowerbeds. Can you find the perfect place for her, near Marigold and Nasturtium?

Marigold Fairy

Nasturtium Fairy

Summer Scene

Here is a wonderful Flower Fairy scene for you to pull out and keep. Use your stickers to make the picture even more beautiful!

pages 2 – 3

pages 4 – 5

pages 6 – 7

pages 8 – 9

page 10

page 11

pages 12 – 13

pages 14 – 15

pages 8 – 9

Picture Perfect

Look at this pretty fairy picture. Can you copy it onto the grid at the bottom by filling in the spaces with stickers?

Fairy Trail

Some Flower Fairies and their friends are meeting today for a fabulous fairy picnic! Each fairy has something to take along. Can you figure out what each fairy brings by following the trails? Then put the right sticker at the end of the path.

Cornflower Fairy

Rose Fairy

Bird's-Foot Trefoil Fairy

Fantasy Fairy Tale

Here is a Flower Fairy tale for you to enjoy, but two of the pictures are missing.
Can you read the story first and then find the missing pictures?

Warm weather has come at last! The Flower Fairies meet in the sunshine and greet each other for the first time since Winter.

There are lots of stories to share and new friends to be made.
Many of the Flower Fairies have wonderful new clothes to wear too! Sometimes the new babies need a little help.

"Let's go for a walk," says Pansy. "There must be lots of new friends to meet in the far meadow. Follow me." The friends skip through the grass together.

Pansy was right. There are lots of new fairies to meet. The warm day has brought them all out to play. "Let's have a party to welcome the sunshine!" says Buttercup.

That evening, when the sun went to bed and the stars came out to play, the meadow was full of laughing Flower Fairies. They danced and sang together until the sun came back again in the morning.

13

Summer Ball

It is almost time for the sparkling summer ball. Can you help these four fairies dress in their party clothes? Use the descriptions of each fairy's outfit to help you find the right stickers.

Columbine

A glittering gown made from petals and a touch of fairy dust! Delicate pink slippers complete her outfit.

Columbine

Strawberry

Strawberry

An emerald green hat that shines in the sun, and sparkly shorts to match his bright top!

Buttercup

A delicate dress
woven from petals
and sparkly sunshine.
Leaf slippers are
snug on her fairy feet!

Buttercup

Bugle

Bugle

Bright blue petals make
a stunning shining hat!
Bugle plays fairy music
at the ball on his horn.

Answers

Winter Magic
page 2-3

Snowdrop   Holly   Winter Jasmine   Hawthorn

A Flying Visit
page 4-5

White Clover visits Honeysuckle

Primrose visits Ragged Robin

Herb Robert visits Burdock

★ Herb Robert passes over the most flowers and butterflies.

Fairy Trail
page 11